Surprising Silhouettes

This book is dedicated to anyone who has a dream they think is out of reach but has *not* given up trying to make it happen.

Surprising Silhouettes

Written and Created by Connie Tamaddon

Nautilus Press

New York   Los Angeles   London   San Diego

Published by Nautilus Press,
a division of The Nautilus Works

Library of Congress Cataloging-in-Publication Data available on request.

ISBN 978-0-9778018-3-1

Library of Congress Control Number: 2010921436

First edition
A C E G I J H F D B

Printed in the United States of America

Have you ever been surprised when you realized that something is *not* what you thought? When an object is lit in a certain way, it becomes an outline or "silhouette" that can be something quite unexpected. I hope you enjoy guessing what these silhouettes really are!

You may think I always land on my feet, but I'm really a sugary treat you love to eat.

What am I?

I'm candy!

You may think I bark and play fetch
for days,
but I'm really covered in sprinkles
and glaze.

What am I?

I'm donuts!

You may think my curly tail might look
like a cork,
but I'm really a food you can twirl on
your fork.

What am I?

I'm pasta!

You may think that I nibble and hop,
but I'm really full of air and might go POP!

What am I?

I'm balloons!

You may think that I slither on the ground, but it's really on your feet where I can be found.

What am I?

I'm socks!

You may think I swim in a school without a sound,
but I'm really something that grows in the ground.

What am I?

I'm flowers!

You may think that cheese is what I crave,
but I'm really something you spend
or save.

What am I?

I'm money!

You may think my favorite meal is flies, but I'm really a healthy treat your parent buys.

What am I?

I'm fruit!

You may think my quills are quite a fright, but I'm really something you use to draw and write.

What am I?

I'm pencils!

You may think that I'm something soft
you can cuddle with at night,
but I'm really something hot out of the
oven and baked just right.

What am I?

I'm bread!

College Track is an after-school program working to increase high school graduation, college eligibility and enrollment, and college graduation rates among low-income, under-resourced high school students. College Track's intended impact is to close the achievement gap and create college-going cultures for students who are historically and currently underrepresented in higher education.

All proceeds from this book will be donated to College Track

COLLEGE TRACK SUPPORTS...

More than 850 high school and college students at centers in East Palo Alto, Oakland, San Francisco, and New Orleans, and has a proven track record of success.

PROGRAMS & SERVICES

All of College Track's programs for high school and college students are centered on four core service areas: Academic Affairs, Student Life, College Affairs, and College Success. For each of these programs we have established a set of clearly defined student goals and expectations mapped to college acceptance requirements and structured to best prepare students for the academic, social, and financial demands of college. Over the course of four years, this support amounts to the equivalent of one extra year of high school.

▶ Academic Affairs: Provides students with tutoring, small-group academic workshops in all subject areas, SAT and ACT preparation, and academic counseling.

▶ Student Life: Enables students to gain leadership skills, be involved in extracurricular activities, participate in cultural and artistic events, and engage in community service.

▶ College Affairs: Organizes college tours and informational sessions with college admission representatives, provides scholarships, and oversees financial aid packages.

▶ College Success: Supports College Track students once they are in college to ensure that they are academically and financially able to complete their degree.

www.collegetrack.org

"I want to go to college because I want to stay away from the violence of the world. As a College Track student, I have learned a lot of what life will expect of me, such as the skills and knowledge I need to be a successful high school graduate and an even more successful college graduate. Thank you all for your support, because without it, my dreams may not be fulfilled."

RESULTS

100% of our seniors graduate high school

▼

Over 90% are admitted to a four-year college

▼

Of the 340 students we have sent to college, 90% are still pursuing or have earned a college degree

▼

88% of College Track students who enroll in a University of California school graduate from college within 6 years

▼

85% of College Track students are/will be the first in their families to graduate college

▼

Over 90% of our students come from low-income households

College Track Oakland
436 14th Street, Suite 500
Oakland, CA 94612
Phone (510) 835-1770

College Track East Palo Alto
1877 Bay Road
East Palo Alto, CA 94303
Phone (650) 614-4875

College Track New Orleans
2322 Canal Street
New Orleans, LA 70119
Phone (504) 620-2332

College Track San Francisco
2398 Jerrold Avenue
San Francisco, CA 94124
Phone (415) 206-9995

STUDENT TESTIMONIALS

"I want to attend college because I want to continue my education, get a job, and make my family proud. I want to take advantage of all that my parents have given me by sacrificing so much and coming to the United States. Neither of my parents completed high school let alone went to college. I will be the first in my family to go to college."

"My reason for going to college is I want to be successful. I want to be successful because I want to prove that I can, even though people may doubt me."

"You only have one shot to make life great and the only way you can do this is by finishing college."

"I want to attend college and stand out from all the drop-outs and people who never tried."

www.collegetrack.org

Silhouettes can be like people. What you first see is just an outline, not the whole person. It takes time to get to know what a person is really like.

Here are some questions to think about:

Why is it important *not* to prejudge others?

Have you ever had someone prejudge you before they got to know you?

Have you ever prejudged someone and found out that you were wrong about that person?

How can we avoid prejudging people?